The Confident Little swan

A Little Animal Adventure

The Confident
Little Swan

Written by Sarah Albee
Illustrations by John Carrozza

Published by The Reader's Digest Association Limited
London ❖ New York ❖ Sydney ❖ Montreal

Little Sandy Swan was peeping through the reeds with her friend, Greta Goose. 'Look at them,' Sandy whispered to Greta. 'They're getting better every day.'

Sandy and Greta were watching Sandy's brothers and sisters at their flying lesson. In just a few weeks, it would be time for the swans to fly south for the winter months. Sandy was the smallest swan in the flock and had not yet begun to fly.

'You can do that too, Sandy!' urged Greta.
'I know you can. You just need to practise and
grow stronger.'

'No, no,' said Sandy, shaking her long neck.
'I really can't do it. I am too small to make the
trip. My mum said she'd stay behind with me.'

'You can't stay *here* for the winter,' said
Greta, looking shocked. 'It's too cold!'

Sandy tossed her head. 'We'll manage,'
she said.

Suddenly Greta had an idea. 'I'll give you lessons!' she honked. 'I'll be your trainer!'

Sandy nuzzled her friend affectionately. 'Thanks, but ...'

'We'll start today,' said Greta firmly, as
Sandy started to say something else. But Greta
refused to listen to her friend's protests.

Sandy sighed. 'Okay, I'll try,' she said. 'But I
can't even get into the air yet! My flight feathers
haven't finished growing.'

Days went by. The first time Sandy tried to fly, she flapped her wings rapidly for a few seconds, but nothing happened.

'I think I saw some lift there. I really do think so,' said Greta, flapping down next to her friend.

'There was no lift,' muttered Sandy sadly, shaking the water out of her feathers.

But soon after that, she did manage to stay airborne for just a few seconds. 'You're doing it! You're flying!' honked Greta excitedly.

Several more weeks went by, and Sandy and Greta practised every day. Sandy's flight feathers were growing rapidly. Although she was still quite a bit smaller than her brothers and sisters, she was starting to fly short distances.

Sandy and Greta took a break from their flying practice to watch Sandy's brothers and sisters. 'They're getting much stronger,' said Sandy admiringly.

'So are you!' said Greta. 'They're going to be so surprised!'

Finally, one day in October, Sandy and Greta were in a distant part of the marsh. Sandy took off across the water, then flew high up into the air, swooping in a wide loop before settling down gracefully next to Greta. Her eyes were shining as she looked at her friend.

'I knew you could do it,' whispered Greta.

'Let's show my mum and dad!' said Sandy.

Sandy's mother and father were talking
together about leaving the marsh for the winter.
'We'll have to say good-bye in the next few
days,' said Sandy's father sadly.

'I wish Sandy had more confidence in
herself,' sighed her mother. 'Where is Sandy, by
the way?'

Suddenly one of Sandy's brothers began
honking wildly. 'Look! Look up there!' he
shouted.

'It's Sandy!' cried all the young swans.
Sandy soared above their heads in a wide loop, her now-strong wings flapping elegantly through the air.

As Sandy landed in front of her family, her mother raced over to her. 'Oh, Sandy!' she said. 'You must have been practising and practising!" 'She certainly looks strong enough to make the journey with all of us,' added Sandy's father.

Sandy looked over at Greta. 'It's all thanks to my friend,' she said. 'She knew I could do it, and she gave me the confidence to keep trying.'

Greta flapped her wings at Sandy. 'See you down south!' she said, and flew off to find her own flock.

All about ... SWANS

FACT FILE

SUN-SEEKERS
Before winter, some swans fly to warmer places where food is easier to find. In the spring, the swans fly back north to raise their young.

BIG BIRDS
The trumpeter swan is the largest of all swans. It can stand 1.8m (6ft) high – as tall as a grown man – and open its wings nearly 2.5m (8ft) wide!

ELEGANT AND USEFUL
The long necks of swans allow the graceful birds to pull up underwater plants to eat, without having to dive.

Did you know?

WATERSKIING SKILLS
When landing on water, swans put their feet in front of them and ski across the surface of the water to a stop.

DRIP-DRY FEATHERS
A swan's feathers are water-proof. The feathers have oil on them so that water just runs off, keeping the swan dry.

WEBBED FEET
Swans have webbing between their toes. The webs act like paddles in the water, helping the swans to swim.

YOUNG FAMILIES

The Confident Little Swan is a Little Animal Adventures book
published by Reader's Digest Young Families, Inc.

Written by Sarah Albee
Illustrations by John Carrozza
Notebook artwork © Paul Bommer

We are committed both to the quality of our products
and the service we provide to our customers.
We value your comments, so please do contact us on
08705 113366 or via our website at
www.readersdigest.co.uk
If you have any comments or suggestions
about the content of our books, email us at
gbeditorial@readersdigest.co.uk

Printed in China

Book code: 637-032 UP0000-1
ISBN: 978 0 276 44361 9
Oracle code: 501800109H.0024